LOOK O LEONARD!

Jessie James & Tamara Anegon

DK

This is the Shrew family.

There's Mr Shrew, Mrs Shrew, Sam, Stevie, Sasha, Sydney, and Leonard...

GOOD DAY TO YOU!

HELLO THERE!

Oh wait, there he is!

YO!

Today is an exciting day for the Shrew family. It's moving day!

They've got a long journey through the forest to their
new home, so Mrs Shrew has asked everybody to hold
on to each other's tails so that they don't get lost.

There they all are.
Can you count them?

5

6

7

"All here!" says Mr Shrew and off they go!

But what's this?
Leonard is holding on
to the wrong tail!

This tail is too thick and
furry to be Sydney's.

LOOK OUT,
LEONARD!

Phew! That was a close one!
And look, there's Leonard's family.

He's not far behind. Maybe he can reach Sydney's tail.

Oh no! That's not
Sydney's tail.

That tail belongs to a
snippy, snappy crocodile!

LOOK OUT, LEONARD!

Yikes! That was a lucky escape.
But where is Leonard going now?

Uh-oh! Leonard has grabbed on to the tail of a slithery snake!

He doesn't look very friendly. **LOOK OUT, LEONARD!**

Oh dear! Leonard had better catch up
with the rest of the Shrew family fast.

There they are! They're greeting their feathery friend, Mr Parrot, on their way past.

Leonard is close behind them. What a relief!

Oh no! That's Mr Parrot's tail!

BOING!

That was a BIG fall!

Phew! What a surprisingly soft landing.

LUCKY LEONARD!

The rest of the Shrew
family aren't far away.

If Leonard is quick, he
could reach them!

There they are!
Leonard is almost there.

Come on Leonard,
you can do it!

But what's this? Leonard's family has met a big, hungry, SCARY tiger!

What are they going to do?

Uh-oh! That
tree branch is
very wobbly!

Leonard is
very high up!

LOOK OUT,
LEONARD!

HURRAH! CLEVER, LEONARD!

But look!

Leonard has knocked off
one of the coconuts...

right onto the
tiger's head!

But how will Leonard get down from the top of that big, tall tree?

LOOK OUT, LEONARD!

There he goes, sliding down that leaf.

WELL DONE, LEONARD!

That was an exciting adventure, but now little Leonard is back with his family. He never wants to get lost again!

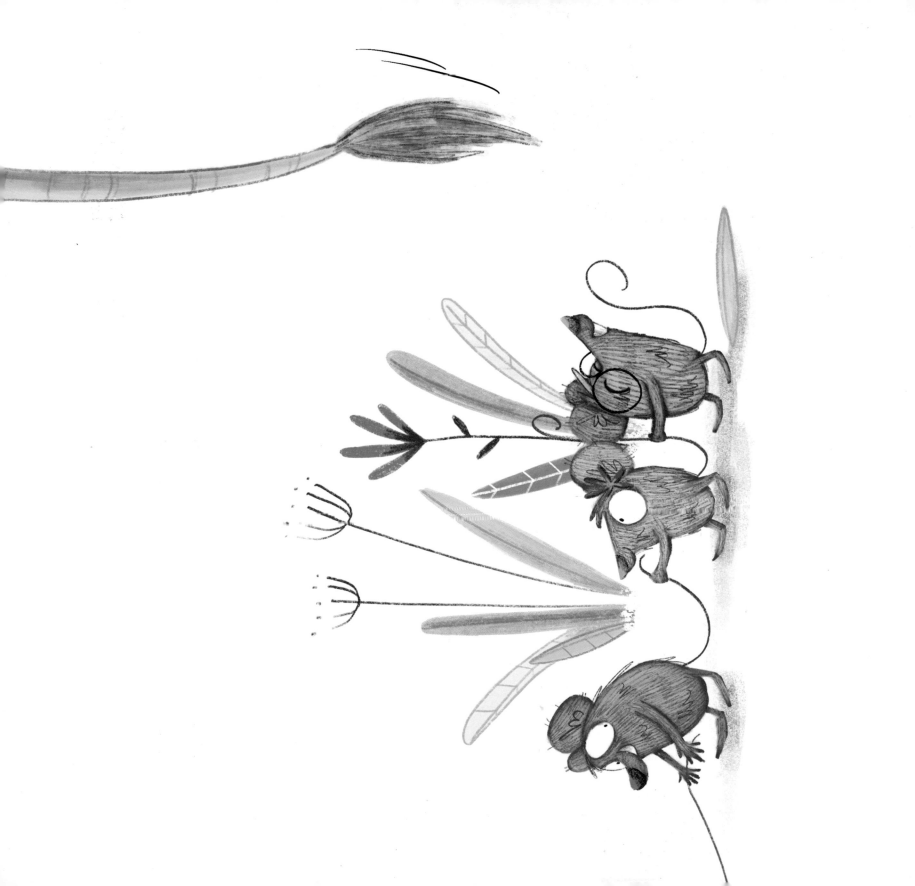

ABOUT THE SOUTHEAST ASIAN SHREW

Measuring at just 8cm (3 in) long, the Southeast Asian shrew is found across parts of Cambodia, Malaysia, China, Laos, Thailand, and Vietnam. These tiny little mammals have soft fur, long tails, sharp teeth, and a pointed snout – perfect for foraging through leaves and grass in search of insects and seeds to eat. Like most shrews, they have big appetites, and need to eat their own body weight in food every day. Because of this, they are active day and night – rarely stopping to rest. Shrews have excellent senses of hearing and smell, but poor eyesight – which might explain why Leonard is always getting into jams!

ABOUT TAMARA ANEGON

Tamara Anegon is an illustrator living in Madrid, Spain. She loves to bring her characters to life in a way that they become her best friends, and Leonard is no exception with his hilarious range of expressions. When Tamara isn't drawing, she can be found dancing to swing music.

Written by Jessie James and illustrated by Tamara Anegon
Created and designed for DK by Plum5 Ltd.

DK | Penguin Random House

Editor Abi Luscombe
Designer Brandie Tully-Scott
Publishing Manager Francesca Young
Jacket Coordinator Isobel Walsh
Publishing Director Sarah Larter
Creative Director Helen Senior
Production Editor Abi Maxwell
Production Controller Inderjit Bhullar

First published in Great Britain in 2020 by Dorling Kindersley Limited
DK, One Embassy Gardens, 8 Viaduct Gardens,
London, SW11 7BW

Imported into the EEA by Dorling Kindersley Verlag GmbH.
Arnulfstr. 124, 80636 Munich, Germany

Copyright © 2020 Dorling Kindersley Limited
A Penguin Random House Company
10 9 8 7 6 5 4 3 2 1
001–321960–March/2021

A CIP catalogue record for this book is
available from the British Library.
ISBN 978-0-2414-6976-7

Printed and bound in China

Mix
Paper from
responsible sources
FSC™ C018179

For the curious
www.dk.com